CATCH A FALLING STAR

a tale from
The Iris the Dragon Series

By Gayle Grass

With Illustrations
By Coral Nault

Iris the Dragon Inc.
Otter Creek, P.O. Box 923
Smith Falls, Ontario,
Canada K7A 4W7
E-mail: info@iristhedragon.com
www.iristhedragon.com

Canadian Cataloguing in Publication Data

Grass, Gayle, 1948-
    Catch a falling star

(The Iris the Dragon series)
ISBN 0-9688532-0-X

    1.Mental illness--Juvenile fiction. 2.Mental health--Juvenile
fiction. I.Nault, Coral, 1948- II. Title. III. Series: Grass, Gayle,
1948- . Iris the Dragon series.

PS8563.R369C38 2001   jC813'.6   C2001-900185-1
PZ7.G772Ca 2001

Printed in Canada by Dollco Printing

Editor: Virginia Mainprize
Computer technician: Chris Woods
Design: amoeba corp. www.amoebacorp.com

Disclaimer: This book contains general information about children's mental health issues. It is not intended as a substitute for the advice of a trained medical professional. Readers should not attempt to diagnose or treat their children based on the material contained in this book, but rather should consult an appropriate medical or psychiatric professional before starting or stopping any medication and before implementing any other therapy discussed in this book. The author and publisher are not responsible for any adverse effects resulting from the information in this book.

Catch A Falling Star

Catch a Falling Star is a fairy story. It begins one summer morning when a boy called Fish is fly-fishing from an old wooden bridge near his home. He casts out his line and reels in a straw hat decorated with flowers. "I think you caught my hat," says a sweet, high voice. And so, Fish meets Iris, a wise and gentle dragon who lives in a cave under the bridge. Fish and Iris become good friends and share exciting adventures. Iris shows Fish the best places to catch fish and she introduces him to the other creatures that live in and along the river. However, Fish, who is beginning to develop some of the early signs of mental illness, feels anxious and confused at times. He tells Iris how he feels and she helps him understand and deal with his illness, teaching him how to relax and telling him her dragon secrets for a healthy brain. When Fish returns to school that fall and his feelings of anxiety continue, Iris suggests that he and his parents seek professional help. After the winter holidays, Fish leaves Iris and his home to spend time in a clinic in the city. He writes to Iris telling her about his life in the clinic. Gradually, with the support of doctors and nurses and because Iris has been looking after and shining his star, Fish begins to become well. In the spring, he returns home to his family and a special surprise.

There is an ancient dragon legend that says that the stars in the heavens are the guiding lights for all living creatures. Dragons know the secret of the stars and have been given the responsibility of keeping them from falling.

CATCH A FALLING STAR

a tale from
The Iris the Dragon Series

By Gayle Grass

With Illustrations
By Coral Nault

Summer

Once upon a time, not that long ago, there lived a boy called Fish. His family and friends had given him this nickname because, more than anything else, he loved fly-fishing.

Fish lived with his mom and dad and his two younger sisters, Sophia and Samantha, in a big stone house on a hill overlooking a small lake. The lake flowed into a river that ran under an old bridge built of logs and rocks. Tall willow trees grew along the shore of the riverbank, and the river was alive with birds and animals.

The bridge was Fish's favourite place. He spent many happy hours there, practicing fly-fishing and dreaming of the river's long, winding journey to the sea. He loved to see how far he could cast his line before it touched the rippling waters below.

Catch a Falling Star

This morning Fish was feeling upset and he didn't know why. He had felt this way more and more lately and it worried him. Again and again, he tried to cast his line out across the water in the graceful arc that he had practiced so often. He couldn't seem to get it right.

Once again he tried, but the line just dropped down into the river and began drifting under the bridge. Fish tried to reel in his line, but it was stuck. He pulled harder, and as the end of his line came into view, he saw that he had caught something strange. When he pulled it closer, he realized it was a straw hat decorated with flowers.

"I think you caught my hat," said a sweet, high voice.

Fish looked around quickly but didn't see anyone. All of a sudden, he heard a loud splash from under the bridge and out swam a green dragon.

"Who are you?" asked Fish, jumping back.

"I'm Iris, a swamp dragon. I live in my cave under this bridge and you took my hat right off my head while I was dozing on my doorstep," said the dragon with a huge yawn.

  Catch a Falling Star

"But I've never seen you before," said Fish, examining Iris more closely.

"You may not have noticed me," said Iris, "but I've often watched you fishing from this bridge. I must say that you're getting very good, although those last few casts were a little shaky. Is something bothering you, Fish?"

"Well, I guess so. I woke up really early this morning and couldn't get back to sleep, so I decided to come and fish. Most of the time I find it very peaceful here, but today I feel restless and keep thinking of other things. I just can't seem to get my cast right. It's making me really frustrated. But Iris, I didn't know there was a cave under this bridge. Can I see it?"

"I can't show it to you, Fish. It's against dragon tradition. Our caves are secret, private places where we go to be alone and think. They are filled with books and treasures that we have collected from all over the world. But come and sit on this log and I'll tell you about myself."

Fish and Iris settled on the log and sat quietly for a few minutes, listening to the river flowing by and to the sounds of the river animals waking up. Fish was beginning to feel more relaxed.

"Iris?" said Fish. "You don't really look like a dragon, you know."

Catch a Falling Star

"But I am a dragon," said Iris. "Look, I even have gold wings. Although they're small, I can fly. You probably think that all dragons have big teeth and long, sharp claws and breath fire. Well, some do, but I don't.

"I'm a swamp dragon and we're different from other dragons. We're actually very kind and gentle. Our symbol, or coat of arms, is the iris, a flower that stands for faith, hope and courage. We try to live by those words. My favourite teacher, Dr. Socrates, taught me the rules that swamp dragons follow," explained Iris. "He is a very wise dragon."

"Iris, I really like my teacher, Mr. Brooke, but I don't always get what he is saying," Fish replied.

"Don't worry Fish, maybe I can help you. Hey, would you like to see some amazing places to fish? Jump on my back and I'll show you where they are," Iris said suddenly.

Fish hesitated, but Iris seemed kind and friendly, and he very much wanted to see these places. So he climbed down from the bridge and onto her bumpy back.

"Hold onto my ears but try not to mess up my new hat. I've just made it," said Iris as she swam out into the river.

Over the next few weeks, Iris and Fish became good friends. Every day, after Fish finished his chores at home, he went down to the bridge to see Iris. Iris showed him the best places to fish and where the ripest berries grew along the shore. Sometimes they went swimming and diving with Iris's friends Ottie Otter and Madeleine Frog. But some of their best times were spent just lying in the soft grass on the riverbank, looking up at the clouds and listening to the bees humming in the flowers. Fish felt a lot less confused and much happier just being with Iris.

At the end of one hot summer's afternoon, Fish and Iris were resting on the riverbank. They had spent most of the day swimming and playing in the water with Ottie and Madeleine. Iris and Fish were both tired but felt happy and relaxed.

Fish suddenly grew serious and asked, "Iris, sometimes my brain gets very busy and noisy and then I get scared. Why is that?"

"Our brain can get sick, Fish, just like the rest of our body. It's important to take care of our brains," Iris replied. "Do you know that we have to exercise the brain? I like to think of it as brain gym. I'm going to tell you my dragon secrets for a healthy brain."

"What sort of secrets?" asked Fish?

"Well, did you know that picking berries is good for your brain?" asked Iris.

"No," said Fish, sounding confused. "How does picking berries help my brain?"

"It exercises your brain parts. Not just picking berries but picking them all sorts of ways, first with your right hand and then with your left, or closing your eyes and feeling for them. Or if you are really talented like me, picking them with your toes," boasted Iris.

"Oh, Iris," giggled Fish, "you have really big feet which makes it easier for you."

"You just have to practice and you will see how talented you can be too," said Iris.

The holidays were coming to an end. The days were a little cooler, and sometimes there was an early-morning mist on the lake.

Very early one morning, Fish arrived at the bridge, just as the sun was rising. He sat down on the log outside Iris's cave. When Iris heard him, she came right out. She noticed that he seemed distracted.

"What's worrying you, Fish?" she asked.

"I'm thinking about going back to school next week and it makes me nervous," Fish answered.

"Why does it make you feel nervous?" asked Iris quietly.

"I can't always understand what my teachers are saying and then they get frustrated with me. The other kids sometimes laugh at me. I'm worried it might happen again this year," said Fish.

"Do you often have trouble concentrating in class?" asked Iris.

"I guess so," sighed Fish. "Mr. Brooke gave me a lot of extra help last year, but sometimes I still had trouble understanding. So my parents took me to our family doctor, Dr. Tay. She talked to me for a long time. I had to do some sort of written tests. She told my parents that I should see a special doctor in the city and maybe I would have to go to a clinic there for awhile. That makes me really frightened."

"I know how you feel, Fish. But sometimes we just can't solve all our problems by ourselves," said Iris. "Sometimes we need help from special people. Don't worry, Fish. Lots of people are helping you and trying to make you feel better," explained Iris. "Now let's go and fish."

Catch a Falling Star

Fall

The summer holidays were over and Fish went back to school. Every morning he waved goodbye to Iris from the school bus as it drove by the bridge. Every afternoon he went down to the bridge to tell her about his day.

The first few weeks of school went well, but one afternoon Fish came to the bridge. "Iris, are you there?" he called impatiently.

Iris was on the riverbank, picking berries and fruit. She was busy getting her pantry filled with food for the winter.

"I'm over here," said Iris. "Come and sit under this apple tree and have a nice, juicy apple. How is school going? You look worried."

"Iris, I can't seem to focus on what my new teacher, Ms. Christie, is saying. I try, but it's so difficult. She thinks I want to disrupt the class."

Iris looked at Fish. "How do you feel at school?"

  Catch a Falling Star

"Sometimes I feel worried and a little anxious and afraid, and I don't know why," Fish tried to explain to Iris.

"Maybe your brain is working too fast again. There are so many things for you to think about at school. You need to help your brain slow down. Remember how relaxed we felt when we were lying on the riverbank, looking at the clouds and listening to the river. I'm going to teach you another way to relax your brain. You can do it anywhere, even at school. I call it dragon breathing. This special way of relaxing has been passed down from dragon generation to dragon generation. We use this skill when we are feeling stressed. It's fun and it really helps me relax and focus. Let's do it together and see if it helps you.

"OK, Fish, put your head back against the apple tree and make yourself comfortable. Now think happy thoughts. Think of how you feel when you're standing on the bridge in the early morning. Everything is so peaceful and calm. Are you ready to practice dragon breathing?"

"Can I learn to breathe fire?" asked Fish, very excited.

"No, Fish, only dragons breathe fire. We don't do it often and have to be very careful that we don't set something alight. You know, Fish, history has given dragons a bad reputation. People think we are bad and they are always trying to slay us for one reason or another. But most dragons are really kind and considerate."

"Now try this. Take a deep breath through your nostrils and as far down into your belly as you can. Blow out hard through your mouth as if you were trying to blow out a candle. As you blow, feel your muscles relax."

"Iris, I don't have wide nostrils like you do and my belly is not nearly so big as yours," said Fish, not quite sure how this was going to work.

"I know, Fish," said Iris. "Dragons have big nostrils so we can breathe deeply and get ourselves under control quickly. When we are worried or afraid, our breathing is shallow and this makes us anxious. Deep breathing helps us relax. Our brains need lots of oxygen to work properly. OK, you try it. Keep your eyes closed and listen to the sound of the wind in the willows and the birds singing. Now breathe. Feel your body relax and your fears go away."

After a few tries, Fish opened his eyes and smiled.

"How do you feel now?" asked Iris.

"Much better. Thanks, Iris, for helping me. I'll try and practice dragon breathing everyday."

Iris put a scaly paw on Fish's shoulder, patted it and said, "We'll practice together. Now, you better get going. It's time for supper and your parents will be wondering where you are."

Fish left for school the next morning, hoping things would get better. He tried to relax as Iris had told him, but during the class he suddenly heard his teacher say, "Fish, what are you thinking about? Your head seems to be in the clouds. You have not finished your assignment. I really don't know what to do with you. You will have to stay in during recess again." Ms. Christie didn't mean to criticize, but she didn't know how to help Fish focus on his work.

Fish heard some of the other children snicker and he felt even more confused. He really did want to try, but why couldn't he keep his mind on what his teacher was saying?

When he got home that afternoon, he jumped off the school bus and ran right down to the bridge.

"Iris, come quickly, I need your help. Where are you?" He started kicking at the logs on the bridge and pacing up and down.

"Fish, I'm here," said Iris, coming up from under the bridge in a hurry.

"I don't want to go to school, ever again," said Fish, shaking all over.

Iris looked worried. She knew something very wrong was happening to her friend Fish. She knew he was showing the early signs of a brain illness, and the stress of school was making it worse. She thought it might be time for him to see a psychiatrist, a special doctor who is trained to help people with brain disorders.

"Fish, do you think you need someone special to help you? I know you are worried about going to the city to see another doctor, but I think you should tell your parents you would like to go. It might help. What do you think, Fish?"

"I don't know, Iris. Will the doctor be like your wise dragon teacher, Dr. Socrates?" asked Fish, thoughtfully.

"Just as wise and friendly, I'm sure. Talk to your parents tonight and see what they say, and I'll talk to Dr. Socrates and ask him what he thinks," encouraged Iris.

  Catch a Falling Star

That night after dinner, Fish's father saw that Fish was worried. "Are you having trouble at school again, Fish?" he asked. "Ms. Christie telephoned me today to say she was concerned about you."

"I guess I am, Dad. I talked to my friend Iris the Dragon and she thinks I should go and see the doctor in the city. I think maybe she's right. She's going to talk to her dragon teacher Dr. Socrates and ask him what he thinks," Fish replied.

"Well," said Fish's father, looking at Fish's mother, "I think you and this Iris the Dragon friend of yours have made a good decision. See what Dr. Socrates says and we'll make an appointment to go and talk to the specialist Dr. Tay suggested we see.

Next morning Fish went down to the bridge to tell Iris what he had told his parents.

"Fish," she said, "I spoke to Dr. Socrates last night and he thinks it is important that you go and see the doctor in the city. He said that getting help from specially trained doctors is a good idea."

Soon the day came for Fish and his parents to visit the psychiatrist. They had never been to the clinic before, and they were all a bit nervous.

Iris watched them drive away and hoped that everything would be all right. She spent the day in her cave, checking her books to see what they said about mental health problems and brain disorders.

It was late when Fish returned, but he came right down to the river looking for Iris.

"How are you, Fish?" asked Iris, as soon as she saw him.

"I'm OK, Iris," Fish answered, "but I'm really tired. It was a long appointment. The doctors and nurses asked me and my parents lots of questions. They took us on a tour of the clinic. They think it's a good idea for me to stay there for a while. They say it will help me understand why sometimes I feel the way I do and help my brain get better. I've decided to go after the winter holidays."

"I know it will help you, Fish. Life is like our river here. It travels a long way, with many twists and turns, but reaching the ocean makes the journey worthwhile," encouraged Iris.

  Catch a Falling Star

Winter

The winter holidays came. There was lots of snow on the ground and the lake was frozen. Fish and Iris spent many long hours skating, sliding down the riverbank on their bottoms and making dragon sculptures. They even did a little ice fishing to keep in practice. Fish felt less anxious and more relaxed and happy.

One very cold night, Iris and Fish had finished skating on the lake and were lying in a snow bank looking up at the sky. Millions of stars twinkled in the blackness.

"Why are the stars so bright tonight, Iris?" asked Fish.

"Because the dragons of the world have been looking after them," Iris answered.

"What do you mean?" said Fish.

"Well, dragon legend says that the stars in the heavens are the guiding lights for all living creatures. Dragons know the secret of the stars and have been given the responsibility of keeping them from falling," replied Iris.

"Do I have a star?" asked Fish.

"Yes, that one peeking just over the top of the apple tree by the bridge. While you're away, I'll keep an eye on it for you. Goodnight, Fish," said Iris softly.

The holidays ended all too quickly, and Fish went off to the clinic in the city. At first he felt a little nervous and lonely, but in a few days he had made friends with some of the other kids.

He really liked the doctors and nurses, too. They helped him understand why he became worried, frustrated and angry at times. They explained that sometimes his brain was not working quite right. They said that the noises he heard in his brain were caused by a chemical problem. And they promised to try to make it better.

Living at the clinic was not that different from being at home. Fish went to school and had chores to do. There was plenty of time to have fun, and Fish and the other kids often went skating and tobogganing in the park. Fish showed them how to make dragon snow sculptures. They reminded him of Iris.

Fish really missed Iris. He decided to write her a letter.

January 24, 2000

Dear Iris,
    I really miss you but I know people here are trying to help me. They say that when I hear noises in my head and get confused, it is a chemical problem in my brain. They are going to help make it better. They are teaching me ways to relax when I get upset and scared. I show them my dragon breathing. They are very impressed. Did you know it's the year of the Dragon on the Chinese calendar? I figured it out that I am a dragon child. I guess that is why we are such great friends. Anyway people here seem to understand what I am feeling. I don't get criticized for what I say and I feel less worried. I still want to be a great fly fisher. I really miss you. See you soon.

Love
Fish

P.S. Are you taking care of my star for me?

Spring

It was spring and the city burst into colour. Tulips and daffodils were blooming in all the parks and gardens. The doctors and nurses felt that Fish was ready to leave the clinic. He was feeling much better and knew what to do when he felt worried and confused.

The day came for Fish to go home. He felt sad about leaving all his friends at the clinic. But he knew that they would keep in touch. At the meeting a few days before, his parents and the staff had talked about how to help Fish's brain stay healthy. The doctors had sent reports about Fish's progress to his family doctor. They had sent a special education plan to his school. And they told Fish's parents to call for advice at any time and to let them know how things were going.

Fish was so excited to be going home. He had missed his sisters and the old stone house on the hill. He had so often thought of the old bridge and the river that flowed to the sea. He hoped that nothing had changed. With all his heart he hoped that his special friend, Iris, would still be in her cave under the bridge.

  Catch a Falling Star

As they rounded the last bend in the road, Fish caught sight of the bridge. He saw the river flowing and the waves gently lapping against the riverbank. The apple tree was covered with white flowers.

The car rattled across the old bridge. Fish noticed tables with coloured tablecloths on the front lawn. As the car stopped in front of the house, the front door flew open. Suddenly a group of people came out, crying, "Welcome home, Fish." It was his family and friends, and even Dr. Tay and Ms. Christie were there. Everyone was really happy to see him back.

Fish had a wonderful afternoon. There were hot dogs and lemonade. There were games and prizes. And best of all, Fish's parents had a special surprise for him – a puppy.

Fish kneeled down and the puppy jumped all over him, licking him and wagging his tail.

"Oh, thank you, I love him," Fish exclaimed to his parents. "Can I take him for a little walk?"

"Sure, but come back soon for dessert. We have a cake to celebrate this special day," said his mom.

Fish ran down towards the river. His puppy followed close behind at his heels.

As he came to the bridge, Fish whispered, " Iris, are you still there?"

"Yes, Fish, I'm still here and I will always be here whenever you need me. I'm so proud of you. I know it wasn't easy to go away to the clinic. You were brave and you worked really hard there to get better. I have a special gift for you," said Iris from underneath the bridge.

"Oh Iris, I'm so glad you are still here. What is your gift?" asked Fish.

"Well, I've been looking after your star and today I gave it a special shine. I've hung it as high in the sky as I can. It's much higher over the apple tree than it used to be. Look for it tonight," whispered Iris. "I see you have a new puppy. What's his name?"

"I think I'll call him Star," said Fish, laughing because the puppy was tugging at his pants.

"You'd better get back to your party," said Iris. "But remember, Fish, you are a dragon child and this is a special year for you. Just keep believing in yourself and know that there are people around to help you. And when you grow up and see a falling star, catch it, shine it brightly, and throw it into the sky as high as you can."

The End

Catch a Falling Star

The Journey: How and Why Iris Was Born

Iris the Dragon is the creation of author Gayle Grass and illustrated by Coral Nault – two women with a common bond. Gayle and Coral each have a child who suffers from a brain disorder. Two years ago, while sculpturing in Coral's studio, Gayle conceived the idea of Iris the Dragon and a series of Iris books.

The books were created to reaffirm the message that mental illness exists, is increasing and needs to be understood better; and to create a tool to help children, parents and educators understand that early detection, risk management and education can help to alleviate, if not prevent, mental illness in children.

Mental illness can be due to a chemical or a neurological disorder. It is not the fault of the child or parents. It is like any other disease and needs to be recognized as such. However, the greatest obstacles in the campaign to better understanding and treatment of mental illness are stigma and fear.

It is the hope that Iris, a fairy-tale dragon, will help to break down this stigma and fear and open the door to a better understanding of mental illness. The fairy-tale format was specifically chosen because this medium disassociates the topic from the real world and allows the reader to see mental illness and its effects on the individual in a non-threatening light. As the great child psychologist Bruno Bettelheim wrote in his book The Uses of Enchantment: "For a story to truly hold the child's attention, it must...be attuned to his anxieties and aspirations: give full recognition to his difficulties...suggesting solutions to the problems which perturb him...and promoting confidence in himself and his future." And as Charles Dickens put it: "The imagery of fairy tales helps children ...(achieve) a more mature consciousness to civilize the chaotic pressures of the unconscious."

The book is not only for children, but also for caregivers and others who deal directly with children, to enhance their awareness of the issues surrounding mental illness. This awareness is essential in ensuring a better future for all children suffering from mental illness. It is the first step in the creation of a national agenda to highlight the areas of neglect and develop models of treatment, research, service, information and advocacy.

Both Gayle and Coral, and all the people who have worked with and supported them in this project, hope that this book will be another tool in ensuring a brighter future for children suffering from brain disorders.

  Catch a Falling Star

Sponsorships and Endorsements

Iris the Dragon Inc. is enormously grateful for the support of the following organizations and individuals without whose help and encouragement this book could never have been completed.

Organizations and Individuals that Have Endorsed this Book

The Federation of Medical Women of Canada (FMWC)

Jacqueline Shannon, Board President, NAMI, the National Alliance for the Mentally Ill

Jacques Bradwejn, MD, F.R.C.P.(C), Professor and Chairman of the Faculty of Medicine, Psychiatry, University of Ottawa

Simon Davidson, M.B., B.Ch., F.R.C.P.(C), Chief of Staff and Chief of Psychiatry, Children's Hospital of Eastern Ontario, Associate Professor of Psychiatry and Paediatrics, University of Ottawa

Health Canada

The Honourable Michael Kirby, Canadian Senate

Peter S. Jensen, MD, Ruane Professor of Psychiatry, Columbia University, and Director, Center for the Advancement of Children's Mental Health. Formerly Associate Director, National Institute of Mental Health, for Child & Adolescent Research

J. Andrew Pritchard, Osler, Hoskin & Harcourt LLP

We also thank Health Canada and The Canadian Academy of Child Psychiatry for their help in distributing this book, and the Children's Hospital of Eastern Ontario Foundation (CHEO) for establishing, and for their continuing support of, The Iris the Dragon Fund to help children with mental health issues. Part of the proceeds from the sale of this book, along with all other donations, will go into this fund.

Order Form

To order a copy/copies of *Catch a Falling Star,* please fill out this order form and mail it to: **Iris The Dragon Inc., Otter Creek, P.O. Box 923, Smith Falls, Ontario, K7A 4W7.** If you have any questions, or want information about discounts on orders of 20 or more books, you can write to us at the above address, telephone: 613-284-2049, fax: 613-283-9507, or email: info@iristhedragon.com

---

Please send me:

Copies of *Catch a Falling Star* @ $15.95 Cdn. $10.95 U.S.   _____

Total cost   _____

Plus $5.00 postage and handling for each address

up to 5 books. Add $1.00 for each additional book   _____

Subtotal   _____

Canadian orders add 7% GST to subtotal   _____

Total amount   _____

Method of payment:

Enclosed is a: Cheque ☐ Money Order ☐ payable to *Iris the Dragon Inc.*

Charge my: Visa ☐ Mastercard ☐ Card # _____ Expiry date _____

Name on the card _____

Signature as on the card _____

U.S. and international orders payable in U.S. funds. Please allow 3-4 weeks for delivery after May 1.

Sold to:

Name _____

Address _____

City _____ Prov./State _____ Postal/ZipCode_____

Phone number(in case we have a question about your order) (   )_____

Ship to: (if different from above) (if sending to more than one address list on a separate sheet)

Name _____

Address _____

City _____ Prov./State _____ Postal/ZipCode_____

Gift card should read _____

Part of the proceeds from the sale of this book will go to the Children's Hospital of Easten Ontario Foundation(CHEO) into The Iris the Dragon Fund to help children with mental health issues.